1-13

M

MY 1ST GRAPHIC NOVEL®

Race on the River

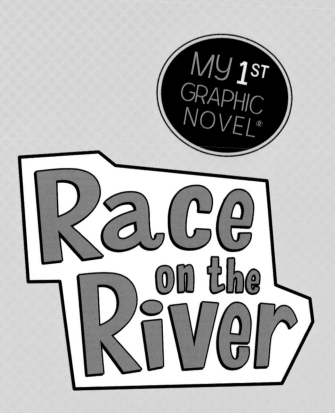

MY FIRST GRAPHIC NOVELS ARE PUBLISHED BY STONE ARCH BOOKS
A CAPSTONE IMPRINT
151 GOOD COUNSEL DRIVE, P.O. BOX 669
MANKATO, MINNESOTA 56002
WWW.CAPSTONEPUB.COM

Library of Congress Cataloging-in-Publication data is available on the
Library of Congress website.

ISBN: 978-1-4342-2521-4 (library binding)
ISBN: 978-1-4342-3061-4 (paperback)

Summary: Mikey's older brother, A.J., is better at everything. When the boys go to
the river for the day, Mikey is determined to beat A.J. in a tube race.

Art Director: KAY FRASER
Graphic Designer: HILARY WACHOLZ
Production Specialist: MICHELLE BIEDSCHEID

Photo Credits: Shutterstock: Paul Clarke, 4, 5; axel2001, 22 (top); Baloncici, cover;
diligent, 6 (top); Dmitry Naumov, 24; Eastimages, 18, 20 (top); ecxcn, 13 (bottom);
Edin Ramic, 14; goran cakmazovic, 15; jean-luc, 19, 20 (bottom); Liz Van Steenburgh, 8, 17;
Mares Lucian, 10; Markus Gann, 7; Skyline, 9, 21; Tatiana Grozetskaya, 6 (bottom), 11;
Tischenko Irina, 13 (top), 16, 25; Valery Shanin, 22 (top), 23 (both)

Printed in the United States of America in Stevens Point, Wisconsin.
092010
005934WZS11

Race on the River

written by **Scott Nickel**   illustrated by **Steve Harpster**

STONE ARCH BOOKS
a capstone imprint

HOW TO READ A GRAPHIC NOVEL

Graphic novels are easy to read. Boxes called panels show you how to follow the story. Look at the panels from left to right and top to bottom.

Read the word boxes and word balloons from left to right as well. Don't forget the sound and action words in the pictures.

The pictures and the words work together to tell the whole story.

Mikey's older brother, A.J., was better at everything. A.J. could shoot baskets better.

A.J. could run faster.

A.J. always got the highest score on video games.

Mikey wondered if he'd ever do anything better than his brother.

The next day, Mikey's family was going to the river.

The river was always fun. Mikey liked watching people race in canoes.

He also liked watching the big paddle boat travel across the water.

At the river, everyone fished. Well, everyone except Grandpa. He mostly slept.

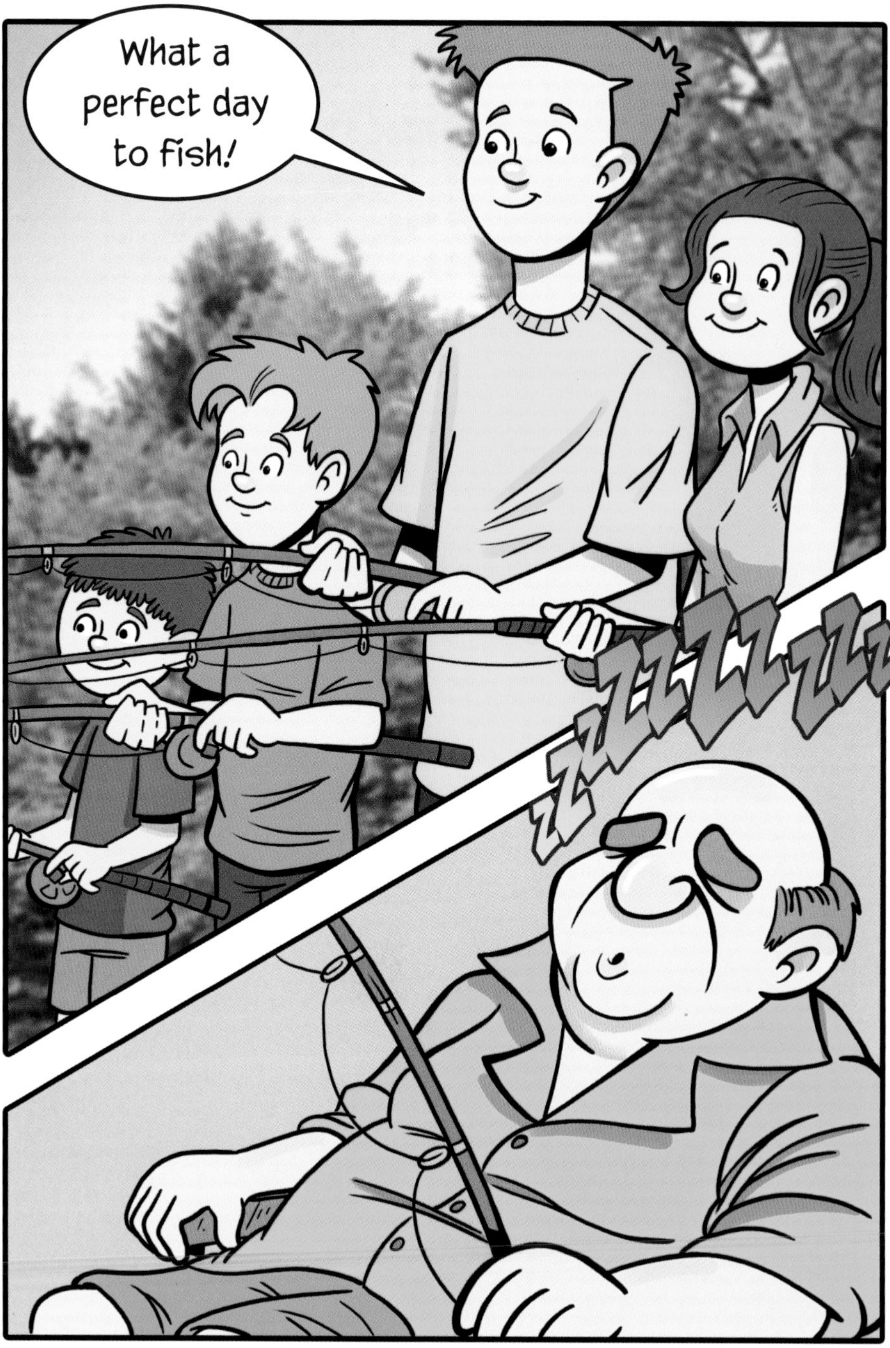
What a perfect day to fish!
zzZZZZzzzz

Mikey felt a tug on his line. He turned the reel faster and faster.

Mikey was so happy. He'd caught a fish.

Then something tugged on A.J.'s line.

A.J.'s fish was much bigger than Mikey's.

Mikey wanted to play on the tree swing. He and A.J. raced to it.

Mikey ran as fast as he could, but A.J. was faster.

Mikey swung high and kicked his legs.

Mikey jumped from the tire. He made a big splash.

A.J. jumped on the swing. He went higher and higher.

A.J. jumped, too. Of course, he made a bigger splash.

Mikey's dad had a surprise. He rented tubes to ride on the river.

Mikey wanted to race. Maybe this time he could beat his brother.

At first, Mikey had trouble with his tube. He spun around and around.

Oh, no!

The strong current carried Mikey and A.J. down the river.

The water pushed the tubes together.

A.J. paddled faster. He passed Mikey and waved.

Mikey's heart sank. He couldn't keep up.

A.J. pulled far ahead. He leaned back in his tube and closed his eyes.

Mikey kept paddling. He saw the big waterfall.

Mikey slowly glided around it.

A.J. didn't slow down. Water poured over A.J.

Mikey was in the lead. He paddled as hard as he could.

Mikey's arms hurt, but he couldn't stop. He was almost at the shore.

Mikey won the race! He finally beat A.J. It was the best river day ever!

BIOGRAPHIES

SCOTT NICKEL has written graphic novels, short stories, nonfiction, and some really good knock-knock jokes. He lives in Indiana with his wife, two sons, and eight cats.

STEVE HARPSTER loved drawing funny cartoons, mean monsters, and goofy gadgets since he was able to pick up a pencil. Now he does it for a living. Steve lives in Columbus, Ohio, with his wonderful wife, Karen, and their sheepdog, Doodle.

GLOSSARY

CANOES (kuh-NOOZ) — narrow boats that are moved through the water by paddling

CURRENT (KUR-uhnt) — movement of water in a river or ocean

PADDLE BOAT (PAD-uhl BOTE) — a boat that is moved by a big wheel

REEL (REEL) — a device on a fishing pole that helps the line go in and out

SHORE (SHOR) — the land along the edge of water

Mikey's River Checklist

There are a ton of fun things to do at the river. After my big day, I can check three things off my list. Only four things to do before I've done everything on my list!

✓ 1. Go fishing (But I still want to catch a bigger fish than A.J.)

✓ 2. Go tubing

✓ 3. Jump off the tire swing (I still need to make the biggest splash, though.)

4. Canoe

5. Kayak

6. Ride the paddle boat

7. Camp

I ♥ FISHING!

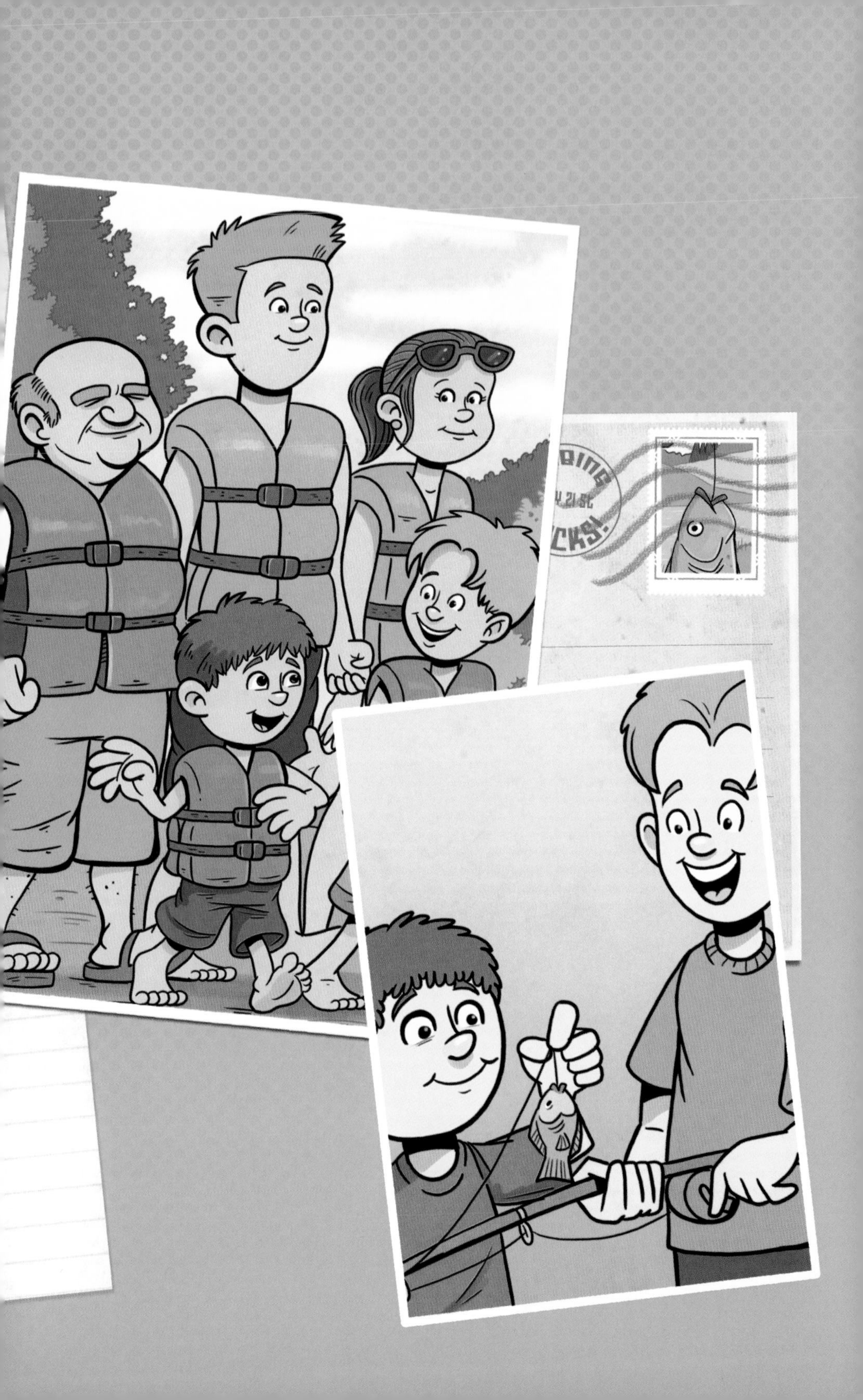

DISCUSSION QUESTIONS

1. Mikey was always losing to his brother, but he never gave up. Why do you think he kept trying?

2. A.J. started the river race with a big lead. Were you surprised by the ending of the book?

3. Do you think A.J. was a good big brother? Why or why not?

WRITING PROMPTS

1. There are lots of fun things to do on the river, like paddling a canoe, tubing, or fishing. Pick your favorite activity, and write a paragraph about it.

2. Make a list of things you would need for a day at the river. Try to come up with at least five items.

3. Write about a race or contest that you have won.